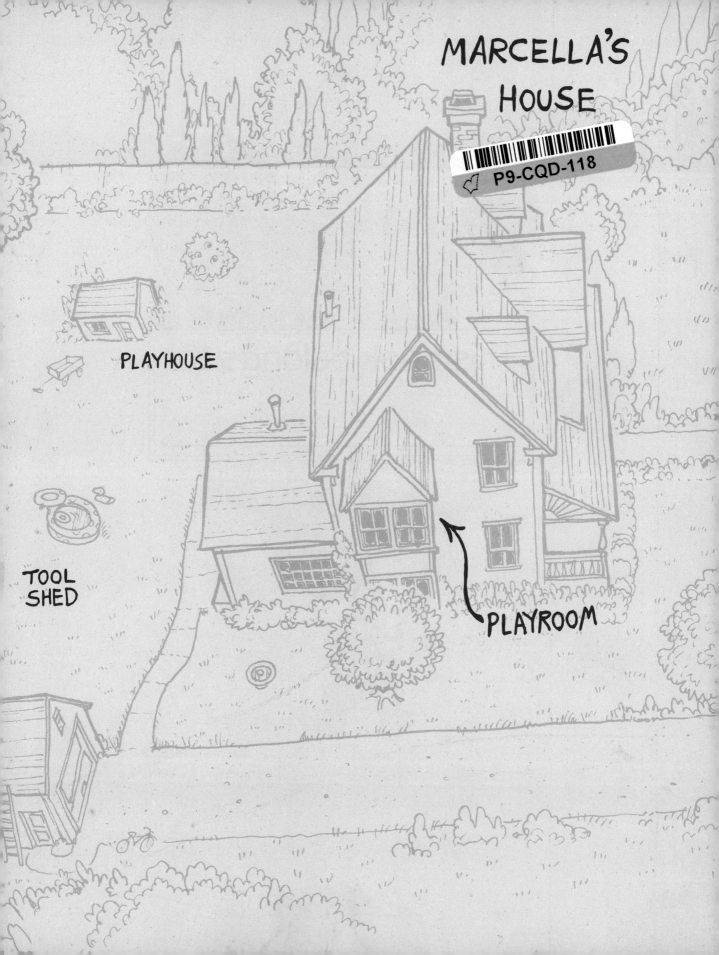

This book belongs to:

_____

Raggedy Ann & Andy's

GROW
AND
LEARN
LIBRARY

VOLUME 17

THE BIRTHDAY SURPRISE

A LYNX BOOK

This book is published by Lynx Books, a division of Lynx Communications, Inc., 41 Madison Avenue, New York, New York 10010. The name "Lynx" together with the logotype consisting of a stylized head of a lynx is a trademark of Lynx Communications, Inc.

Raggedy Ann and Andy's Grow-and-Learn Library, the names and depictions of Raggedy Ann, Raggedy Andy and all related characters are trademarks of Macmillan, Inc.

It was a special day in Marcella's playroom. The Camel with the Wrinkled Knees was celebrating his birthday! That was why Marcella was taking him out to spend the afternoon in the park.

The Camel was very excited. He looked forward to swinging on the swings and sliding on the slide.

"Good-bye now," Marcella called to the other dolls as they headed for the door. "We'll see you later."

"I hope The Camel has a wonderful time in the park today," said Sunny Bunny after Marcella had closed the playroom door.

"I hope he gets to ride on the carousel," said Tallyho the Wooden Horse. "That would be a very special treat."

"That gives me an idea," said Raggedy Ann. "Let's plan something special for The Camel when he gets home. Let's plan a birthday surprise!"

"That's a great idea!" exclaimed Raggedy Andy. "But what could the surprise be?" he wondered.

"How about a drum?" suggested Tim the Toy Soldier. "Maybe we could make a drum for him. That would be a great surprise!"

"No, no—I have a better idea!" shouted Greta the Dutch Doll. "Maybe we could practice a Dutch song, and The Camel could dance to it when he gets home."

"I know!" barked Raggedy Dog. "We could wrap up one of my bones. The Camel could chew on it or bury it in the backyard when he gets back!"

Bubbles the Clown Doll spoke up next. "Hey, maybe we could find something that The Camel could use for juggling," said Bubbles as his floppy arms tossed his own brightly colored balls into the air.

"Wait a minute!" said Raggedy Ann. "I think that we are all thinking about what is special to us, not to The Camel. We need to remember whose birthday it is!" she reminded them.

"I've got it!" shouted Raggedy Andy. "Why don't we make a birthday card from all of us!"

"Yes, we could make it with beautiful colored paper!" said Greta. She and Bubbles ran to get paper and scissors and tape.

"Raggedy Cat and I can draw a picture of The Camel on the front," said Raggedy Dog.

"That's a wonderful idea," agreed Raggedy Ann.

"I'll get the crayons!" offered Tallyho.

"Percy and I will paint 'Happy birthday' on the inside,"
said Tim as he and Percy the Policeman Doll took paint and
brushes off the shelf.

Just then a big smile spread across Babette the French Doll's face. "I know what I can do," she told them. "I'll go to the backyard and pick some beautiful wildflowers. We can give The Camel a bouquet of flowers along with the card!"

"That would be lovely," they all agreed.
"You can depend on me to pick the prettiest flowers in the yard," said Babette as she rushed out the door.

Babette headed right for a patch of sweet-smelling wildflowers in the far corner of the yard.

"Won't The Camel be happy when we hand him a great big bunch of beautiful flowers?" Babette said to herself as she walked along the garden path. "It will be a beautiful bouquet. I'll make sure I find a flower in every single color."

As Babette bent to pick the first flower, a butterfly fluttered in front of her.

"How lovely!" Babette said aloud. She chased the pretty creature, calling out, "Where are you going, little butterfly?"

Soon the butterfly flew over the fence and out of the backyard.

Babette climbed through the hole in the fence and followed the butterfly right into the Deep Deep Woods.

"Hi!" her friends the sparrows called, and she waved as she happily ran by them.

Back in the playroom, the dolls were busy working on the birthday card.

Greta and Bubbles were hard at work cutting the paper to just the right size for the card.

"Do you think this is big enough?" Bubbles asked, holding the paper up for Greta to see.

"Yes, Bubbles," Greta giggled. "I think you could have made two or three cards with all that paper!"

"The card will be terrific," Raggedy Andy said.

"Yes, I think The Camel will be very pleased when he sees what we have made for him," agreed Raggedy Ann.

"And he'll really like the flowers, too," Sunny Bunny added.

"Look at all the beautiful colors we used," said Raggedy Cat.

Sunny Bunny added some hearts. "That's because The Camel is so special to us," he said.

Everyone admired the card. Raggedy Andy looked up
at the clock. "Where is Babette?" he wondered aloud.

At that very moment, Babette was following the butterfly into an open meadow.

"Oh, I could play with you all day," Babette laughed as she chased after her new friend.

The afternoon began to slip away, and Babette thought only of the beauty of the butterfly and the fun she was having in the meadow. She completely forgot that her friends were counting on her to pick the flowers that would make The Camel's birthday extra special.

Meanwhile, Percy the Policeman Doll and Tim the Toy Soldier were almost finished painting the birthday message on the card.

"Happy Birthday to Our Friend Camel. We All Love You Very Much!" is what they wrote on the inside.

Everyone agreed that this was a fine thing to write on a birthday card.

"Now we should clean up," said Raggedy Ann when they were finished, and the others began putting things away.

"I hope Babette gets back soon with the flowers!" Raggedy Andy said.

"Where could she be?" the dolls all asked.
"If she doesn't get back soon, our surprise will be
ruined!" cried Sunny Bunny.

Just then Babette returned to the playroom.

"I had the most wonderful time," she told them. "I met a beautiful butterfly, and we played and played."

"But what about The Camel's flowers?" asked Raggedy Andy.

The smile disappeared from Babette's face. "Oh, no!" she whispered, her voice trembling. "I guess I sort of—well, the butterfly—I forgot all about the flowers!"

"But we were depending on you," Tim grumbled.

"I feel terrible," she told them. "I know I let you all down. I let The Camel down, too."

At that moment they heard the front door open. "Quick! Hide the card!" Raggedy Ann said.

"I hope you had as much fun as I did today," Marcella said to The Camel as she placed him back on the bed in the playroom. Then Marcella left the dolls alone.

"I did have a very nice day in the park," The Camel told the other dolls. "We went on the swings and the slide. We even went for a ride in a rowboat, and I got to go on the carousel! Today was certainly a very special birthday."

After The Camel had finished talking, Raggedy Andy spoke up. "Your birthday isn't over yet!" Then he and the rest of the dolls all shouted "Surprise!" while Greta and Bubbles pulled out the birthday card.

"We made this card specially for you, Camel," said Raggedy Ann. "Happy birthday from all of us!"

The Camel didn't know what to say. He was very happy that his friends had made a card for him. "Thank you. Thank you all," he said as he admired the beautiful card.

"Here is one more surprise!" said a little voice from across the playroom. The little voice belonged to Babette. She came from a corner of the room where she had been quietly working.

"This is for you, too," Babette said shyly, handing The Camel a bouquet made from her favorite special ribbons.

The others gasped.

"We were going to give you real flowers, but I hope you like this just as much," Babette said to him.

"It's beautiful, Babette," said The Camel. "And I love this bouquet even better than real flowers because you made it yourself from your own special ribbons. Thank you all. This was the best birthday a camel ever had!"

Raggedy Ann smiled at The Camel, then at Babette. "Sometimes we all make mistakes," she said, "but it's nice to know that we can always depend on each other when it really counts."